COLOR DANCE

ANN JONAS

Greenwillow Books · New York

For my favorite dance troupe, Doninamy

Greenwillow Books, a division of
HarperCollins Publishers,
195 Broadway,
New York, NY 10007.
Manufactured in China by
South China Printing Co.
First Edition
15 16 17 SCP 20

Library of Congress
Cataloging-in-Publication Data
Jonas, Ann. Color dance.
Summary:
Four dancers show how colors
combine to create different colors.
[1. Color–Fiction.
2. Dancing–Fiction] I.Title.
PZ7.J664Co 1989 [E]
88-5446
ISBN 0-688-05990-2
ISBN 0-688-05991-0 (lib. bdg.)

Watercolor paints were used
for the full-color art.
The text type is Futura Bold.

This is our dance.

Red

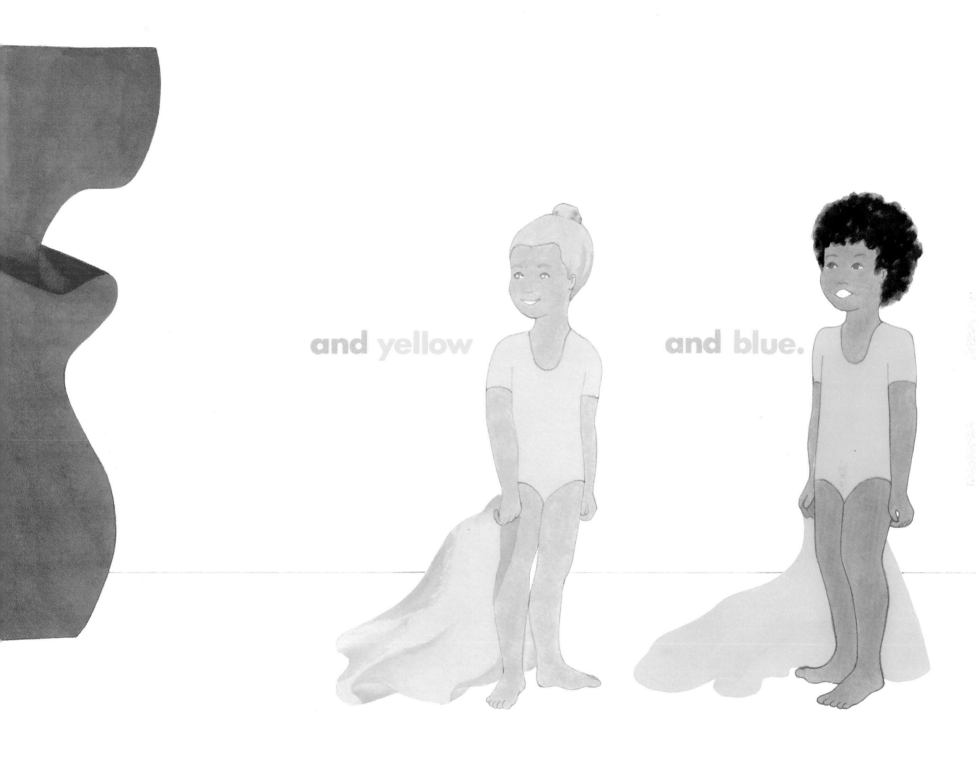

and yellow   and blue.

Orange is **red** and yellow mixed together.

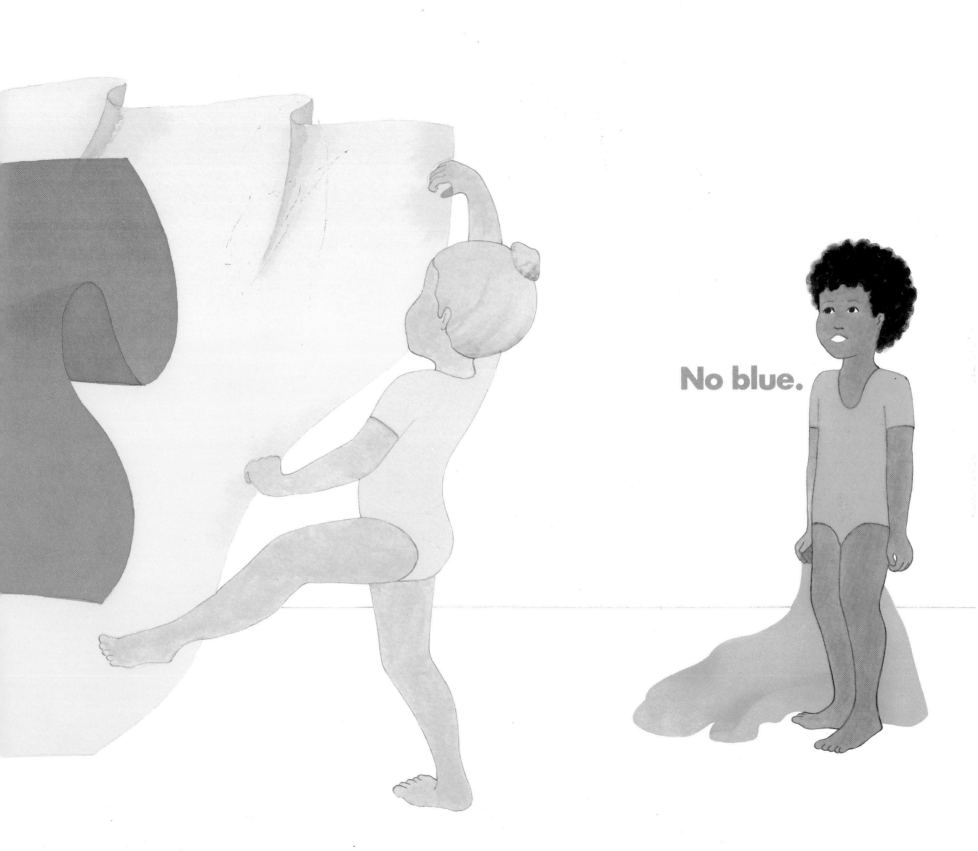

No blue.

Green is yellow and blue mixed together.

No red.

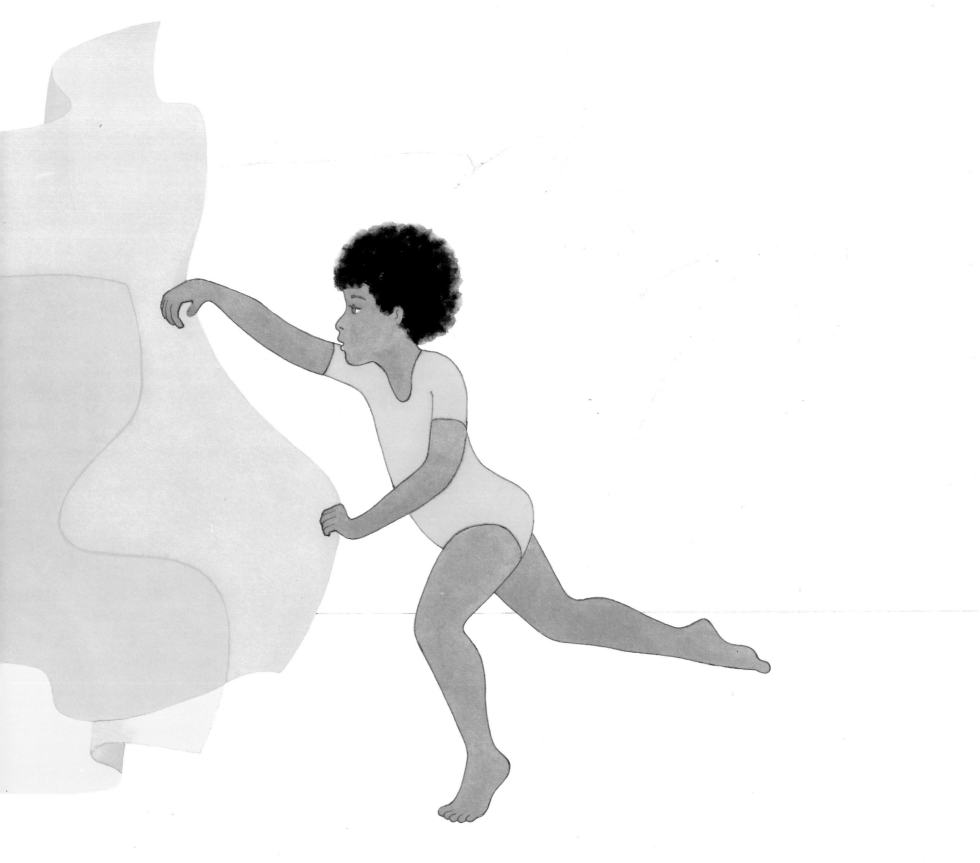

Purple is red and blue mixed together.

No yellow.

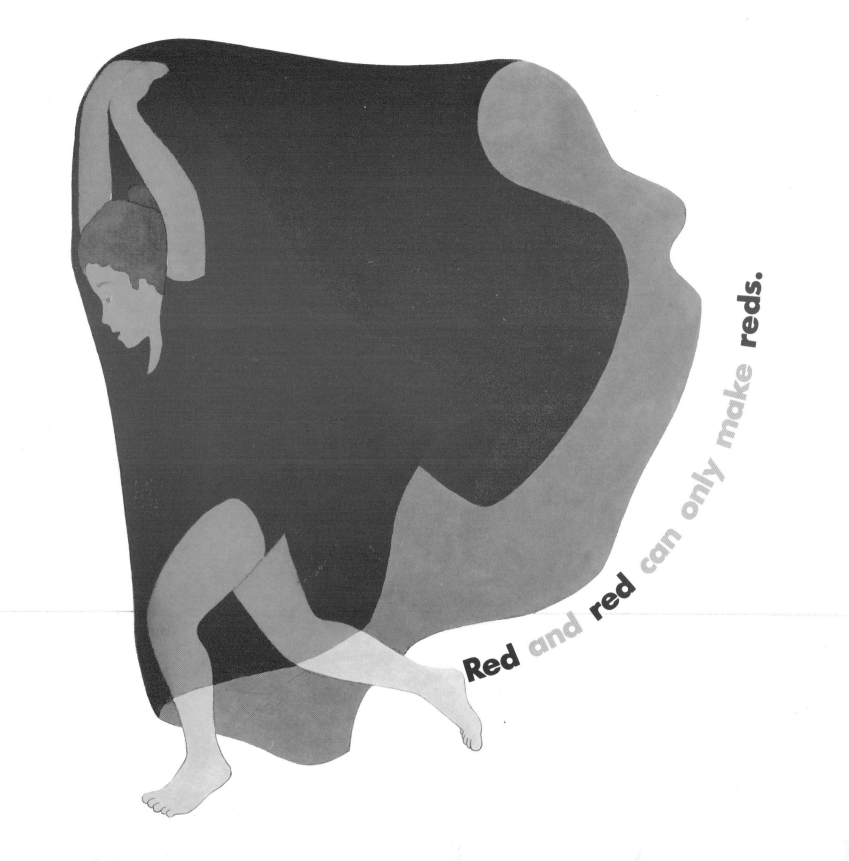

Red and red can only make reds.

Yellow and blue can make
chartreuse
and green
and aquamarine.

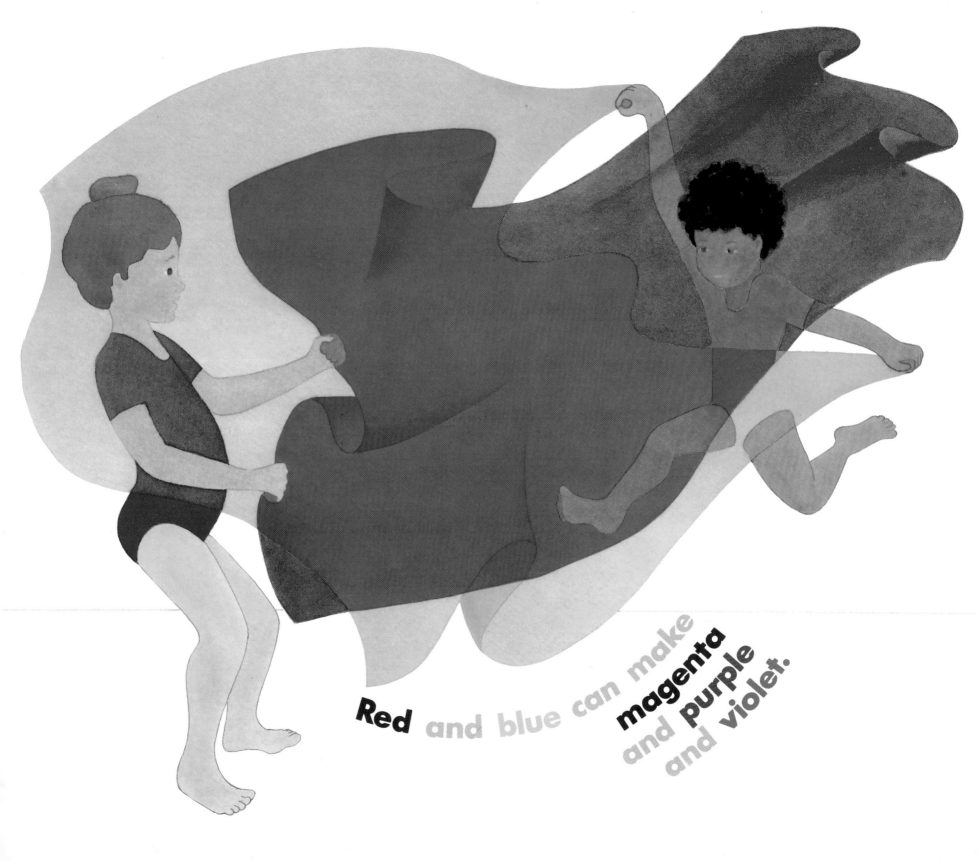

Red and blue can make **magenta** and **purple** and **violet.**

**But yellow
and yellow
can only make
yellows.**

Blue and blue can only make blues.

But yellow and **red** can make marigold and orange and **vermilion.**

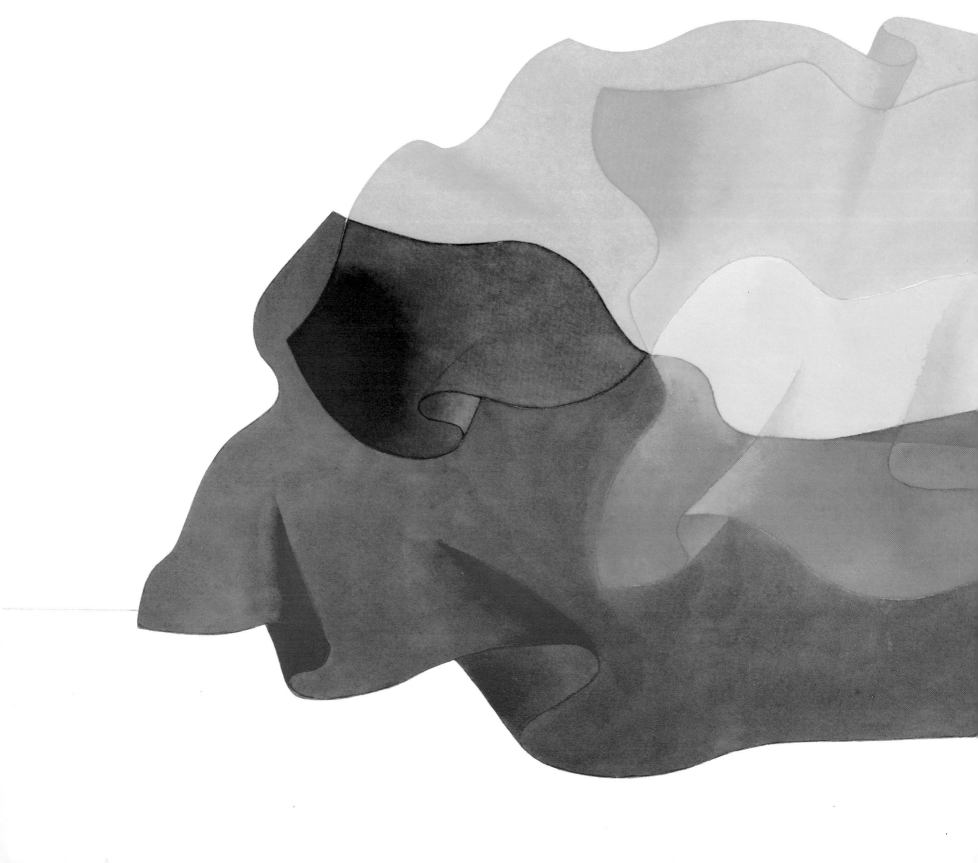

Blue
aquamarine
green
chartreuse!

Yellow
marigold
orange
vermilion!

Red
magenta
purple
violet!

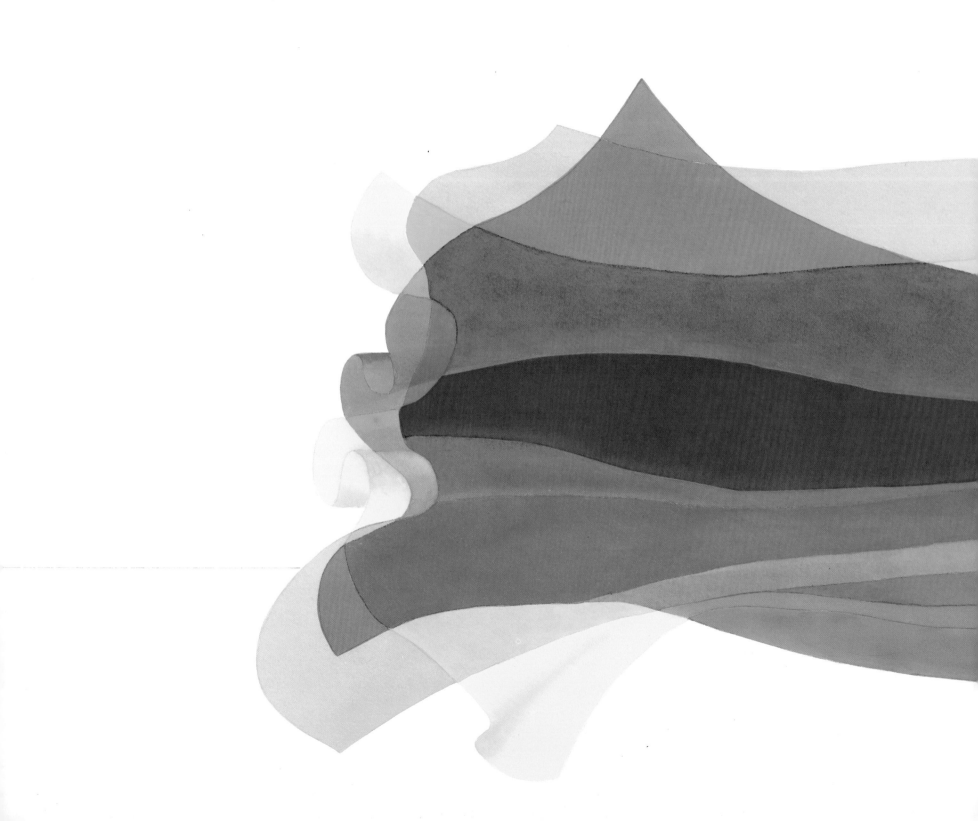

Mix
them
all
together
and
they
make
browns
and
grays.

White makes colors pale.

Gray makes them dark.

Black makes them almost disappear!

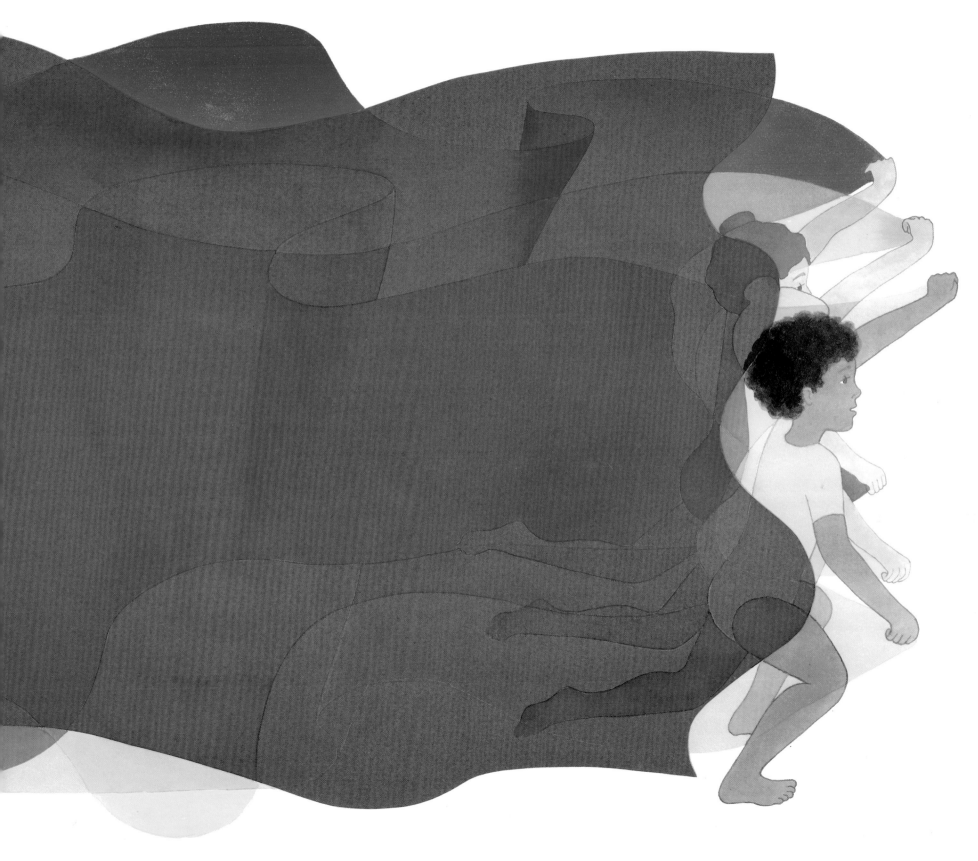

The color wheel below shows the relationships between colors. The primary colors (red, yellow, and blue) are equally spaced around the wheel. Halfway between them are the secondary colors (orange, green, and purple). Between the primary and secondary colors are the combinations of adjacent colors, the tertiary colors. Complementary colors are directly opposite one another. Since mixing all three primary colors will produce brown, gray, or black, so will mixing complementary colors, because a pair of complementaries contains all three primaries.

<u>Color Dance</u> is a fantasy, easier to perform on paper than on a stage. The cleanest mixed colors will be obtained by using pure primary colors—those that do not contain any of the other primaries. The colors used in this book were chosen with that in mind. The red does not have any noticeable yellow or blue in it, nor does the yellow or blue contain any of the other two primaries.

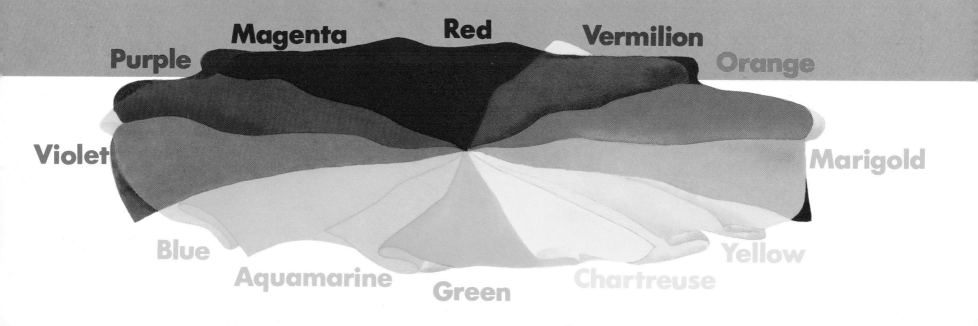

Purple   Magenta   Red   Vermilion   Orange

Violet   Marigold

Blue   Aquamarine   Green   Chartreuse   Yellow